THE LITTLE FIRE DRAGON

Written by Bing Bo

Illustrated by Wu Bo

CARDINAL
MEDIA

This is a story of long ago.

One winter, it was terribly cold.
The thick snow fell and fell, as if it
wanted to cover the whole world.

All the villagers tried to stay warm by huddling with their families at home. They had to ration their firewood, as they wouldn't have enough to cook with if they burned it all for warmth.

"Cruel winter, please go away…" they plead, as their voices trembled with the cold.

But winter didn't go away.
The sun started to grow more
and more faint, slowly turning
white, like a large, dead fish
eye hanging in the sky.

"Oh no! The sun's fire
is going out!"

All the rivers and streams had frozen solid. Families had to wander further and further to find wood. When fires were lit, the families gathered near, gaining a little bit of warmth and a little bit of hope.

In the deepest mountains of the north lived a little fire dragon and her mother. The mother's tail had been hurt and she couldn't fly.

"Mommy, the sun is going out," the little fire dragon said.

"Yes," she said, looking up into the sky. "I'm unable to reignite it from here. Daughter, you'll need to relight it."

"Do you think I can, Mommy?"

"The fire you have in your belly won't be
enough to light up the sun," her mother said.
"You'll have to go to the village and eat the
people's fires, too. It will be dangerous—as
they will be frightened of you. But don't hurt
the humans. Be brave, my girl."

"Yes, Mommy," the little fire dragon said
as she flew toward the village.

When the little fire dragon went through a window into the first house, she scared the people inside half to death.

"Excuse me, but I need to eat your fire to be able to relight the sun," the little fire dragon said. But she soon realized the people couldn't understand her language. She started gulping down the flames. The people shouted at her, telling her to go away

At the next house and the next, the villagers tried to chase her away, beating her with sticks and throwing rocks at her.

She could have easily burned down their houses with a small breath, but she remembered what her mother had told her, so she ate the fires as quickly as she could.

After she went through the village, she had
enough flame within her to relight the sun.
She took a moment to rest, as it would take
all of her strength to fly up to the sun. And
while her wounds hurt terribly, she felt
worse that the villagers didn't understand
she was doing this to help them.

The villagers looked up, with hearts full of despair. It was the middle of the day, but without the sun's light, it was as dark as the night. They were so cold, without fires in their homes.

Suddenly, they saw the little fire dragon flying up into the sky. She flicked her tail back and forth, and swam upward through the air, towards the sun. Only then did everyone understand. The dragon had eaten their fires to help them—to light up the sun!

As the villagers rejoiced, they cheered and called out to the dragon, "Thank you, fire dragon! Yay, fire dragon! We're sorry, fire dragon!"

The little fire dragon flew close to the sun. She opened her mouth, and a long, blazing stream of fire roared out. *Whoosh!* The sun lit up and burned with a blazing red light! The bright rays lit up the whole world, bringing life and warmth to everyone.

The villagers cheered and called out their
thanks to the little fire dragon as she flew
home with her last bit of energy.

"Mommy, I lit up the sun!"

"Yes, my child. You did very well. You were very brave."

"And I didn't hurt anyone."

"Yes, child, I saw that too."

And the mother dragon held her daughter close as the young fire dragon fell asleep, exhausted from the journey.

The sun's rays brought spring to the people below. The snow melted, the grass grew, and the world reawakened.

Each year at springtime, the villagers build a big bonfire to celebrate the fire dragon. They sing songs of her bravery and how she relit the sun, saving the world.